Going for a Drive

Poems by Wendy Cope
Illustrations by Charlotte Middleton

Collins

Contents

Going for a Drive

We are going for a drive.
We are glad to be alive.
Right then, people, off we go.
Vroom, vroom, vroom and cheerio!

Fields and hedges, hills and trees.
Feel the sunshine. Feel the breeze.

Vroom, vroom, vroom, we're on our way.
Vroom, vroom, vroom. Hip, hip hooray.
We are going for a drive.
We are glad to be alive.

Dancing

Look at us, look at us, dancing and dancing
And dancing and dancing the morning away.
Swirling and twirling until we are dizzy,
Don't interrupt us because we are busy.
Swirling and twirling and dancing and dancing
And dancing and dancing the morning away.

Running Around

We like running,
Running around.
Running, running,
Running around.
Faster, faster,
Everybody run.
Then fall down on the ground.
Aagh!

We like jumping,
Jumping around.
Jumping, jumping,
Jumping around.
Higher, higher,
Everybody jump.
Then fall down on the ground.
Aagh!

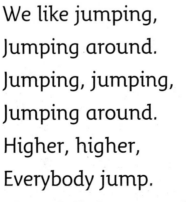

5

Here's a Little Foot

Here's a little foot.
What shall we do with it?
Lift it up
And into the shoe with it.

Into the Bathtub

Into the bathtub,
Great big splosh.
Toes in the bathtub,
Toes in the wash.

Soap's very slidy,
Soap smells sweet.
Soap all over,
Soap on your feet.

Rinse all the soap off,
Dirt floats away.
Dirt in the water,
Water's gone grey.

Out of the bathtub,
Glug, glug, glug.
Great big towel,
Great big hug.

19

Song of the Big Toe

Heigh ho,
Big toe,
To and fro,
Nice and slow.

Pick me up,
Swing me high,
Big toe
Won't cry.

Into bed,
In we go,
Bye, bye,
Big toe.

20

Goodnight

I've snuggled down. I'm ready,
All safe and sound in bed.
My rabbit and my teddy
Are here beside my head.

I've had my bedside story.
Switch off the bedside light.
I'm going sleepy-snory.
It's time to say goodnight.

21

A poetry journey – from morning till night

We've got umbrellas, you and I.
If it rains, they'll keep us dry.

Swirling and twirling until we are dizzy

Right then, people, off we go.
Vroom, vroom, vroom and cheerio!

Swoosh, swoosh, summer toes,
Paddling in the sea.

My mummy said,
"Don't jump in the puddle."

Into the bathtub,
Great big splosh.

I've had my bedside story.
Switch off the bedside light.

Ideas for reading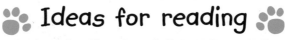

Written by Clare Dowdall BA(Ed), MA(Ed)
Lecturer and Primary Literacy Consultant

Learning objectives: explore how particular words are used, including words and expressions with similar meanings; engage with books through exploring and enacting interpretations; speak with clarity and use appropriate intonation when reading and reciting texts

Curriculum links: Art and Design: Portraying relationships; Music: Play it again – exploring rhythmic patterns

Interest words: illustrations, haiku, cheerio, shimmering, chatterbox, appetite, cocoon, emerged, gorgeous, heigh-ho

Word count: 904

Resources: ICT, the Poetry Archive website, photographs from children's holidays

Getting started

- Look at the front cover together. Read the title *Going for a Drive* and discuss where the people in the car might be going and why.

- Read the blurb on the back cover with the children. Emphasise the rhythm and rhyme of the poem.

- Turn to the contents. As a group, read through the contents list together. Explain that each heading is the title of a different poem.

Reading and responding

- Ask children to choose a poem from the contents that they like the sound of to read to a partner. Children should practise reading their poem quietly before sharing it with their partner.

- Listen as children read and perform their poems to each other. Praise the the use of expression and enthusiastic reading and ask partners to comment on what they like about the performance and how the performance can be made even better.

- Choose a longer poem that hasn't been selected yet, e.g. 'Talking'. Read the poem aloud to the children twice. Discuss the effect of the poem, e.g. how does it make the children feel, what does it remind them of? Discuss the features of the poem, e.g. the use of rhyme, rhythm and powerful vocabulary.